My Life As a
Belching Baboon ...
with Bad Breath

Tommy Nelson® Books by Bill Myers

Series

SECRET AGENT DINGLEDORF
. . . and his trusty dog, SPLAT 🐾

The Case of the . . .

Giggling Geeks • Chewable Worms
• Flying Toenails • Drooling Dinosaurs •
Hiccupping Ears • Yodeling Turtles

The Incredible Worlds of Wally McDoogle

My Life As . . .

a Smashed Burrito with Extra Hot Sauce • Alien Monster Bait
• a Broken Bungee Cord • Crocodile Junk Food •
Dinosaur Dental Floss • a Torpedo Test Target
• a Human Hockey Puck • an Afterthought Astronaut •
Reindeer Road Kill • a Toasted Time Traveler
• Polluted Pond Scum • a Bigfoot Breath Mint •
a Blundering Ballerina • a Screaming Skydiver
• a Human Hairball • a Walrus Whoopee Cushion •
a Computer Cockroach (Mixed-Up Millennium Bug)
• a Beat-Up Basketball Backboard • a Cowboy Cowpie •
Invisible Intestines with Intense Indigestion
• a Skysurfing Skateboarder • a Tarantula Toe Tickler •
a Prickly Porcupine from Pluto • a Splatted-Flat Quarterback

THE IMAGER CHRONICLES

The Portal • The Experiment • The Whirlwind • The Tablet

Picture Book

Baseball for Breakfast

www.Billmyers.com

the incredible worlds of
Wally McDoogle

My Life As a Belching Baboon ... with Bad Breath

BILL MYERS

Illustrations by Jeff Mangiat

Tommy nelson™
FOR TWEENS AND TEENS

A Division of Thomas Nelson Publishers
Since 1798

www.thomasnelson.com

Published in Nashville, Tennessee, by Tommy Nelson®, a Division of
Thomas Nelson, Inc. Visit us on the Web at www.tommynelson.com.

Tommy Nelson® books may be purchased in bulk for educational, business, fund-raising, or sales promotional use. For information, please
email SpecialMarkets@ThomasNelson.com.

Scripture quotations in this book are from the *International Children's
Bible*®, *New Century Version*®, © 1986, 1988, 1999 by Tommy Nelson®, a
Division of Thomas Nelson, Inc. All rights reserved.

ISBN 1-4003-0634-5 (hardcover)

Printed in the United States of America
05 06 07 08 09 WRZ 9 8 7 6 5 4 3 2 1

For Heinz Fussle:
Who knows where real joy lies.

"It is more blessed to give
than to receive."

—Acts 20:35

Contents

Chapter 1

Just for Starters

Celebrating Christmas at my home is like throwing raw meat into a shark tank. We've definitely given a new definition to the term . . . **FEEDING FRENZY.**

It's like when we come down the stairs at 6:00 a.m. on Christmas morning, everything is neat and pretty with a zillion packages under the tree. By 6:01 paper is flying, boxes are ripping, and kids are pushing, screaming, and crawling over one another to get to the goodies.

All this is accompanied by the warm season's greetings of my brothers and sister:

"Get your hands off my present before I break them!"

"Five bucks? That's all Grandma sent me, five lousy bucks?!"

"A used shirt? You gave me another one of your used shirts?!"

"Hey, at least this time I washed it."

Then there's Dad. He's usually sitting off to the side watching with a sick smile on his face—while all the time calculating costs and mumbling, "All these gifts . . . how am I going to pay for all of these gifts . . ."

Finally, there's Mom. She takes so many flash pictures you'd think we're having a lightning storm . . . while all the time shouting, "Save the bows!" "Oh, that is *soooo* precious!" "Brock, stop stomping on your brother and just ask him to pass your presents."

"Ah, Mom . . ."

"I'm serious, you step on Wally's face one more time and you're going to your room!"

Yes sir, for my family, Christmas is definitely the season to be greedy.

Until this year . . .

Now, I'm no great detective, but this year I suspected things were going to be just a little bit different. My first clue was that by Christmas Eve, there still wasn't a single gift under the tree. Come to think of it, THERE WASN'T EVEN A TREE!

(Sorry, didn't mean to shout.)

But Christmas without a tree (or 1.3 gazillion gifts under that tree) is like a surfer without an ocean, a pilot without a plane, or me going to school without tumbling down the stairs, blowing up science labs, or any of the thousand other things required for me to hold the national title of All-School Walking Disaster Area.

I tell you, if I hadn't made a scene a few weeks earlier about buying some cargo pants and my new $150 pair of tennis shoes, the entire month of December would have been a bust.

Even at that, things were not looking good. Not good at all . . .

"What do you think is going on?" my little sister Carrie asked that Christmas Eve as we headed up the stairs for bed.

"I don't know," I grumbled.

"Do you think . . ." She gave a brave little swallow. "Do you think maybe they forgot?"

"Forgot? How could they forget?" shouted Burt, one of my superjock twin brothers, from the sofa where they were watching a football game. (They're always watching football games.) "How could anyone forget? Stores have had their displays up since the Fourth of July."

He had a point. Of course, also there were our Christmas stockings.

"And look," I said as I motioned to them hanging over the fireplace, "they remembered to put up our stockings."

"Did anybody check them?" Carrie asked.

Brock, my other superjock brother and Burt's

twin, nodded. "Nothing but these stupid bottles of sunscreen." He pulled a bottle of sunscreen from his pocket.

"Sunscreen?" Carrie sighed. "Why would we need sunscreen in the winter?"

"Skiers and snowboarders always use sunscreen," Brock explained.

"But we've never skied or snowboarded in our lives," Burt replied.

"We haven't?" Brock asked.

Carrie and I exchanged nervous looks. (Being a superjock doesn't always make you supersmart.)

We continued up the stairs.

"I just don't know what Mom and Dad are thinking," Carrie said.

"Maybe they're not." I muttered.

Suddenly, she looked very frightened. "You mean they're becoming like the twins?"

I shook my head, trying to comfort her. "Relax. Not using your brain is different from not having one."

"Hey," Brock shouted, "I resemble that comment." At least that's what I thought he said. It was hard to tell for certain by the way he was gulping down the sunscreen.

Carrie and I stopped, not believing our eyes.

He paused a moment to catch his breath and

make a face. "I tell you, this is the worst sun-screen I've ever tasted."

"Uh, Brock?" I asked.

"*BELCH?*" he belched.

"I think that's supposed to go on the *out*side of your body, not the inside."

"The outside?" He scowled, then looked at the bottle for directions. "How do you know? It doesn't say."

I shrugged and started back up the stairs. "Just a lucky guess."

Unfortunately, by the next morning, our luck had run out. . . .

* * * * *

"Africa!" I cried. "We're going to Africa?!"

"That's right," Dad said. He pulled the car to a stop outside a giant airplane hangar at the airport.

Mom unfastened her seat belt and explained. "We're spending a week working with a relief agency."

"A week!" we all shouted in four-part harmony (which sounded a lot like four-part misery).

"That's right." As she opened the door, she gave a sweet smile that suddenly succeeded in successfully stimulating all my suspiciousness.

Translation: Mom and Dad were up to something . . . and it didn't sound good.

"Where are our suitcases?" Carrie asked.

"I packed you an overnight bag."

"An overnight bag for a whole week?!"

"Don't worry, you'll have enough underwear to get by."

"*Underwear??* What about the rest of my clothes?!"

"You're wearing them."

"I'M WHAT?!"

But that wasn't the only surprise.

"What about the football games?" Burt asked as we climbed out of the car.

"Yeah," Brock said. "Did you make sure the hotel has satellite and big-screen TVs so we can watch them?"

"They have no satellite or big-screen TVs where we're going," Dad replied.

"How do we watch the games?!"

"They have no games, either."

"No games!!"

Dad shrugged. "It's hard to play games when they're busy starving to death."

I was definitely not liking the sound of this. Nervously, I reached for Ol' Betsy, my laptop computer, then asked, "But the hotel, it has Internet, right?"

Dad nodded. "I suppose."

I felt a wave of relief.

"But we won't be staying in a hotel."

My wave of relief turned into a storm of panic.

"Where are we going to be staying?!" Carrie cried.

Before Dad could answer, someone shouted to him from inside the hangar. "Hey, Herb! We're in here, dude!"

We turned to see this cool-looking guy with a blond ponytail motioning for us to come inside and join him.

"You're just in time to start loading the plane," he shouted.

"We have to load our own luggage?" Carrie whined as we headed toward the hangar.

"No, Sweetheart." Mom smiled. "He's talking about our bringing food on the plane."

"We're expected to bring our own meals?!" Brock complained.

"Not exactly," Dad said as we entered the hangar and a cargo plane the size of Detroit came into view. "We're expected to load the plane with the food we're taking to feed the starving."

* * * * *

The good news was, we weren't the only ones who had to load the plane. Besides the guy with the ponytail (his name was Diggers), there were two or three other workers.

The bad news was, besides the two or three other workers, there were two or three thousand pounds of food! All stacked in boxes. All waiting to be loaded.

"Shouldn't take more than a few hours," Diggers said. He gave me a hand dolly, and we walked up a ramp toward stacks and stacks of boxes.

"What type of food is in there?" I asked.

"Just the basics for survival."

"You mean chips, soda pop, and candy?"

"Uh, no. More like dried biscuits, dried jerky, and powdered protein mix."

I scowled. "Sounds pretty boring."

"They don't think so."

"What do you mean?" I asked as we arrived at the boxes.

"Struggling to survive is anything but boring," he answered.

I nodded. At least this was something I understood. As the Master of Disaster, I'm always struggling to survive. Especially when folks give me dangerous objects to play with like hand dollies and boxes.

And how are hand dollies and boxes dangerous? (You just had to ask, didn't you?)

In the hands of mere mortals, they aren't dangerous. But in the hands of someone with my incredible skills, it's a whole other matter.

"Go ahead and start loading these onto the plane," Diggers said.

I nodded and began:

FIRST—I slipped the dolly under the stack of boxes. No sweat, no worries.

SECOND—I tipped the stack of boxes back onto the dolly. They were heavier than they looked, which called for plenty of:

"ERGs," "ARGHs," and "UMPHs!"
(Lots of sweat, but still no worries.)

THIRD—I rolled the stack down the steep ramp, trying unsuccessfully to keep it under control.

"AUGHHHHHHH . . ."
(Now might be a good time for that *worrying*!)

Before I knew it, I was zipping down the ramp faster and faster . . . and faster some more.

No problem, except for—

"LOOK OUT!" I shouted at Brock, who was pushing his own stack just ahead of me.

K-BAMB

Well, he had been pushing his own stack just ahead of me. Now he and his stack were scattered all over the floor behind me.

"COMING THROUGH!" I shouted at Burt. He was pushing his empty dolly back up the ramp in front of me until

K-SLAM
"WALLLLLLLYY . . ."

he was sailing high into the air above me.

I finally reached the bottom of the ramp, traveling at 1.2 bazillion miles an hour.

The good news was, there was a stack of the boxes looming just ahead like a gigantic wall.

The bad news was, gigantic walls of boxes aren't always the softest to

K-SMASH

into headfirst.

The badder news was, when you *K-SMASH* into gigantic walls of boxes headfirst, you tend to

stagger-stagger-stagger

around until you finally

K-Thud

onto the floor totally unconscious in an I'll-just-lie-here-till-someone-finds-a-doctor kind of way.

Chapter 2

Going UPPPP

The good news was, I didn't stay unconscious forever.

The bad news was, I didn't stay unconscious long enough.

When I woke up the plane was loaded and everyone was ready to go.

Mom and Dad had already called our family doctor—the one who waits by the phone 24/7 for just such McDoogle mishaps. Granted, it costs a bundle for him to be on standby, but he's not nearly as expensive as the extra emergency room the hospital built for my frequent visits.

He came to the airport and did his usual check-Wally-out routine,

   —which, of course, meant I begged him to
     find something wrong,
   —which, of course, meant he didn't,

12

—which, of course, meant my luck was as
bad as ever.

Before I knew it, we were on a plane flying
for twenty-two hours to some country in Africa.
Not, of course, without a few comments from my
brothers and sister:

"Where's the in-flight movie?" Burt demanded.

"Where are the peanuts?" Brock complained.

"How come there's only one bathroom?" Carrie
asked.

Diggers patiently explained, "We need as
much room on the plane as possible to bring in
as much food as possible."

"I don't get it," I said. "Why don't these people
just get a job and buy food like everyone else?"

"Because there is no food for them to buy."

"You're kidding."

He shook his head. "Every day in the world,
24,000 people die from starvation."

"You're kidding."

"That's 1,000 people every hour."

"You're not kidding."

"In fact, in the time it takes me to say this
one sentence, someone else has just died from
starvation."

"Is that why Mom and Dad are taking us?"
Carrie asked. "So we can help?"

"That's part of it," he said.

"Is there more?" I asked.

He nodded.

"Like what?"

"Like getting you to experience the joy that comes from helping folks in terrible need."

I was about to reply when the plane suddenly gave a violent lurch and I

*K-thudd*ed

to the floor and

*roll . . . roll . . . roll*ed

back until I hit a wall of boxes.

I'd barely gotten to my feet before there was another lurch, followed by another mandatory

K-thud

and my

*roll . . . roll . . . roll*ing

to the front.

"Wally," Diggers shouted, racing to me, "are you all right?"

"Oh, sure," I said, resetting my usual broken bones.

As I spoke, a red light suddenly came on in the cabin.

"What's that?" I asked.

"The pilot turned it on."

"Is it like a fasten seat belt sign?"

"Uh, not exactly," he said. "It's a warning to put on our parachutes."

"PUT ON OUR PARACHUTES!"

"Relax, Wally," Diggers said, chuckling as he crossed to a closet and opened it up. "It's standard procedure whenever these old planes hit major air turbulence."

He passed out parachutes to the family and helped us strap them on.

"You're sure we'll be okay?" Dad asked.

"Absolutely."

And he might have been right, except for the part that involved me. Actually, it really wasn't my fault. I mean, how was I to know that just by pulling this one little cord

K-WHOOOOSH
"WALLY!"

my chute would suddenly open up inside the plane.

Luckily, they had a couple of extra parachutes, which allowed me to put on the second one and

K-WHOOOOSH
"WALLY!"

accidentally open it.

And a third.

This time there was no *K-WHOOOOSH* and no "WALLY!" The reason was simple. My brothers had grabbed my arms, pinned them to my sides, and carried me back to my seat where they buckled me in nice and tight.

After thanking them for their thoughtfulness and freeing my arms, I reached for Ol' Betsy. We still had a long way to go. So I started a superhero story, hoping it would keep me out of trouble until we landed. . . .

It had been another grueling day of work for Rhyming Dude McDoogle. As the world's worst rhymer, he'd just created a new ad slogan for a cigarette company:

Put our smoke in your chest,
So we can bring you closer to death.

Then there was the help he gave his favorite rapper, Ice Sleaze. They were working on one of those I-loved-you-but-now-I-hope-you-get-run-over-by-a-bus songs:

Oh, baby, baby,
You slay me,
Make me crazy,
You crush me and mush me,
Like mashed potatoes and gravy.

The second verse was even more genius:

But since you done kicked me out,
I gots to mention your mouth.
Though you be the one I choose,
From your hair down to your shoes,
Your breath stinks worse than
    gym socks—
As bad as my kitty-cat's cat box.

Yes sir, imagine doing all of that work before lunch. Then there was Rhyming Dude's afternoon of writing political slogans for that sneaky governor, Robert Peabody:

If you can trust Robert Peabody...
you can trust anybody.

And let's not forget the reelection
campaign button he wrote that read:

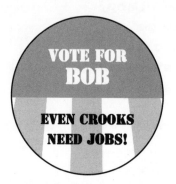

VOTE FOR
BOB

**EVEN CROOKS
NEED JOBS!**

All in all, it had been a great day.
Now our hero is ready to relax when
suddenly there's a tremendous *RUMBLE-
RUMBLE-RUMBLE* like a giant earthquake.

Only there's no giant earthquake,
just a giant earth tilt. That's right,
the entire floor of his house suddenly
turns on end, and he slides all the
way into the

K-Thud

far wall. Actually, it's not the sliding that's the problem, it's the

K-Boom, K-rash, K-Tinkle

of everything else in the house land-ing on top of him that smarts a bit. Everything else, including—

"AUGHHHH..."

his giant-screen TV that is coming right at him. And just when it appears he's going to be a star on that TV screen (or at least a very big SMUDGE), it

K-Zap

disappears. That's right, the entire TV is gone.

Suddenly, the Rhyme Phone rings,

Ding-ding-aling
Ring-a-ring-ding.

(What did you expect a Rhyme Phone to sound like?)

Unfortunately, there's more.

> *ding-dong-dang*
> *ring-rung-rang*

Luckily, before it continues, our hero finally crawls through the junk to answer:

> "Good evening. You got the dimes,
> We'll sell you the rhymes."

> "Good evening, Rhyming Dude."

The chilling call sends a clammy cold through our ultracool character.

> "Material Man! Is it true?
> The one who is calling,
> Is it you?"

The baddest of bad boys can only shake his head at the terrible rhymes. "Of course it's me," he answers. "Who else would Wally use as a villain if he's traveling to Africa to feed the poor?"

"Hey, how'd you know I was going there?" I typed.

"Because we're in your imagination." Material Man sighs. "We know everything you know."

I swallowed nervously. "Everything?"

"Everything."

I swallowed again. "Even the time I was three and wet my——"

"**Especially that!**" he said. "**Now, can we get on with the story?**"

"Oh, sorry, sure . . . ," I typed.

"**Material Man!**" our hero shouts:

"**Are you the reason my house has been jilted?**
Are you the cause for it now being tilted?"

Material Man nods. "I'm the reason the entire country has tilted."

"**Oh, no,**
Say it ain't so!"

"**It's so, Midget Mind. I've just moved to California where I invented my latest weapon of greed. I call it the——**

(May I have some bad-guy music, please?)

Ta-da-DAAAA...

"Thank you. I call it my 'Give-Me-It-All Beam.'"

"The Give-Me-It-All Beam?
Please, tell me,
What does that mean?"

"It means it tracks down everything I don't own and beams it to me so I can—"

"Excuse me?" I typed again.

"What is it now?" Material Man asks.

"You even know about the time my pants accidentally fell down during show and tell in kindergarten and—"

"We know *everything*. Now, may we continue?"

"Oh, sure. Sorry."

I returned to Ol' Betsy and typed Rhyming Dude's response:

"You haven't answered my question.
I need a confession.
Why are things jilting?
Why are we tilting?"

"Because...the weight of all the things I'm gathering is sinking the entire West Coast, causing the whole country to tilt. And that means I'll have to fight a superhero."

"You're calling
Because you're falling?"

"I'm calling because all bad guys in these stories have to fight a superhero. And, anyway, I hate your terrible wannabe Dr. Seuss rhymes."

"But Dr. Seuss, he's my hero.
Without him, life would be zero!"

"Whatever." Material Man sighs. "The point is, if I have to fight a superhero, why not you? That way I'll not only win, but I can also stop your awful rhymes. Now, meet me in Hollyweird at high noon."

"High noon!
That's way too soon.
I live too far away
To travel there in one—"

"Here, let me help." Through the phone our hero suddenly hears:

BEEP BOP.

"What are you doing?
My body, it's moving!"

"That's right!" The bad boy grins.
"It seems that with all of my posses-
sions I don't yet own a superhero who
makes awful rhymes."
    "You mean——"
    "That's right, I'm zapping you over
to join me."

"You can't do that!
Heroes don't get zapped!
Help me, help me, author Wally!
Make your villain stop this folly!"

I nodded and reached for the DELETE key.
(To tell you the truth, I was getting pretty sick
of the rhymes myself.) But suddenly, the plane
gave the second-biggest

K-BOUNCE

of all time. (The biggest is coming up in just a
second.) It was so big that Ol' Betsy flew off my
lap and into the aisle.

Of course, I had to retrieve her,

—which meant unfastening my seat belt,
—which meant getting up,
—which was fine until we hit the world's biggest

K-BOUNCE
(I warned you it was coming)

and I went flying toward the back of the plane.

Unfortunately, this time I missed the boxes and flew past them.

Unfortunatelier, I hit the emergency door at the back.

Unfortunateliest, when I got up, I grabbed the handle, accidentally gave it a yank, and even more accidentally found myself, you guessed it:

"AUGHHHH!"*ing*

as I flew out of the back of the plane and into the night.

Chapter 3

Going Doooown

Luckily, all that practice of opening parachutes inside airplanes finally paid off.

And as soon as I was done screaming my head off and passing out in fear a couple dozen times, I pulled the rip cord.

I heard the chute rushing out of my bag and a moment later felt it open

"OAFF!"

with the world's second-biggest jerk.

(The world's first-biggest jerk was hanging from the parachute still screaming his head off and—I'm not too big to admit it—crying for his mommy.)

But Mom was nowhere around. Come to think of it, nothing was anywhere around. It was just me, a few bazillion stars, and an orange crescent moon in the night sky. Kinda beautiful and peaceful when you stop to think about it.

Kind of crazy and terrifying when you're living it!

(I'm screaming again, aren't I? Sorry.)

I looked down and saw a silver thread of a river reflecting in the moonlight. It twisted and wandered under some majestic treetops.

They would have been more majestic . . .

—if I wasn't falling straight toward them,
—if they weren't coming at me so fast,
—if there was some way I could find the brakes and stop myself from:

K-rash
"AUGHhhh . . ."
SNAP! CRACKLE! POP!
POP! CRACKLE! SNAP!

Those, of course, are the ever-popular sounds of someone falling through African treetops while breaking off several African tree limbs (and a few American Wally legs) in the process.

And then, just when I was sure I was going to hit the ground and turn this into the shortest ever *My Life As . . .* book, my chute got snagged and hung up on a branch, so I

"OAFF!"*ed*

all over again until I

K-SWUNG . . . *K-lunk!*ed

into one particularly hard and unyielding tree trunk, which caused me to, you guessed it, pass out all over again.

(Some habits can really be hard to break.)

Still, as we've already learned from my previous passing-out routines, good times never last forever.

* * * * *

Before I knew it, I was conscious again. When I opened my eyes, I was hanging from the tree. My parachute lines were all tangled up, and I gently swung back and forth, about a hundred feet above the ground. Off to my left was a giant cliff with a river at the bottom.

Everything was still very dark, and I was still very much alone.

—Well, except for the hundred flies and an
   assortment of insects buzzing around me.
—Well, except for the mysterious chirps,

squawks, and howls of African nightlife all around me.

—Well, except for the *rustle, rustle, rustle* in the treetops all around me.

The *rustle, rustle, rustle* in the treetops all—

No, I will not yell again. There's been too much screaming in this book already. I will face my fate like a man . . .

—no matter how loud the rustle.

—no matter how close the snapping branches.

—no matter how red and beady the eyes.

Red and beady eyes!

(Sorry, I don't do red and beady eyes very well.)

I just hung there, staring in stunned silence. Well, the stunned part was right. It's hard being silent when you're bawling like a baby and begging God to let you live (or at least to let you go home and put on some clean clothes before meeting Him in heaven).

But nothing worked. Not even promising to be nice to my little sister for an entire week. (I would have promised more, but lying to God isn't such a good idea—especially if you're about to meet Him wearing dirty clothes.)

Suddenly, the red and beady eyes were no longer around me.

Now they'd dropped directly in front of me!

Not only that, but they were upside down and holding a banana.

Of course, I did what I do best:

"AUGHhhh!"

And, of course, the owner of the eyes answered back. But instead of practicing my brand of communication (which involves plenty of fear and the usual cowardliness), Baboon Boy tried a whole other approach. He opened his mouth and let out the world's biggest

"BELCHHHHHHHH!"

Talk about gross, talk about disgusting. It sounded exactly like my brothers when they're gulping sodas and watching a football game.

Unfortunately, Monkey Man didn't smell as good as my brothers. (Hard to imagine, I know.) I don't want to be rude or say the critter's breath was bad, but just imagine what it's like smelling a skunk in your PE locker . . . who's eaten garlic and onions . . . who's wearing those smelly gym socks you haven't seen since Thanksgiving . . .

who's been dead since Halloween . . . and who has on that awful aftershave you gave your dad for his birthday.

Talk about air pollution! Talk about a toxic waste dump! Talk about panicking and doing everything I could to get away from him!

First, I kicked and twisted and squirmed. When that didn't work, I squirmed and twisted and kicked.

The good news was, I suddenly heard a loud

*K-REEEAK*ing.

The bad news was, it belonged to the branch just above my head—the one my parachute was hung up on.

I looked down at the ground thinking my squirming, twisting, and kicking wasn't such a hot idea after all. In fact, I instantly became very fond of holding absolutely still.

Yes sir, that made a lot of sense.

Unfortunately, my baboon buddy, who was still hanging upside down in front of me, didn't think so. Instead, he had so much fun terrifying me with his first belch, he tried it

"BELCHHHHHHHH!"

again.

But I was made of stronger stuff than that. I wasn't about to panic. I wasn't about to scream. I wasn't about to—all right, maybe just a little

"Augh . . ."

After all, what could a little

"Augh . . ."

hurt? Unfortunately, plenty. Because once again I heard that old, familiar

K-REEEAK . . .

and looked up just in time to see the branch

K-SNAP!

off. This, of course, would explain my sudden falling, my sudden screaming, and the sudden

K-TH . . .

(I didn't get to hear the last *UD* part. It's hard hearing all of a *K-THUD* when you're lying unconscious on a jungle floor.)

Chapter 4

Follow the Bouncing Wally

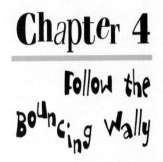

So there I was, minding my own business in the Land of Unconsciousness, when I suddenly felt a warm breath panting on my face . . . followed by a bunch of whiskers tickling my skin.

I figured it was Collision, the family cat. She's always sticking her nose in my face, particularly after I've had a fish dinner the night before.

Of course, I tried pushing her aside, but my ol' body wasn't quite awake yet. No problem. I figured after parachuting out of a plane, landing in trees, chatting with baboons, and falling to some very hard African ground, my body was entitled to a little extra rest. After all—

Wait a minute! How could Collision have followed me all the way to Africa? (And when did I have a fish dinner?)

It was about then that I decided it might be a good idea to open my eyes—you know, just to see what nightmare I was living in now.

But when I opened them, I saw it was no nightmare. It was worse! I was staring right into the face of . . . not a cat, but a dog! And not your normal, everyday, backyard killer variety. No sir, that would be way too normal and everyday. Instead, this little Fido was your ugly skin-and-bones variety, who had some very sharp fangs.

An ugly skin-and-bones variety who looked exactly like those laughing hyenas you see on the National Geographic channel. Only this guy wasn't laughing. Instead, he was licking his nice sharp fangs and anticipating biting into a McDoogle morsel!

I immediately took charge and screamed hysterically.

He immediately leaped back and snarled viciously.

I tried to talk, but it's hard speaking when your heart has relocated to your throat.

He crouched lower, growling, showing teeth so yellow they cried out for one of those tooth-whitening strips.

After several more attempts at speaking, my voice finally kicked in with an all-powerful, totally in charge: "Nice doggy, doggy, doggy . . ."

I heard another growl and spun around to see two more of the critters trying to sneak up on me from behind.

Not wanting them to feel left out, I repeated my greeting, throwing in a few more whimpers and plenty of whines. "Nice doggies, doggies, doggies . . ."

They crouched, snarling with teeth so pointed and ugly they could have signed up for the Vampire Family Dental Plan.

Unsure what to do, but not wanting to be anyone's dog food, I slowly rose to my knees.

They growled louder, not thrilled that their midnight snack was trying to get away.

"Listen, fellas," I half squeaked, half croaked, "I'd love to stick around, but I've got this thing about dying. I mean, I break out in a bad case of death every time it happens."

They weren't impressed with my logic and inched in closer.

I rose to my feet, doing my best to stand strong—though it's hard to stand strong when your legs are as wobbly as Jell-O on a blade of grass in a hurricane . . . during an earthquake.

The good news was, I stood a lot taller than them.

The bad news was, they could solve that by chewing off a couple of my legs.

Ever so carefully, I unhooked myself from the parachute and took a step backward.

Ever so carefully, they took a step forward.

I took another step backward.

They took another step forward.

It was like a weird dance. But instead of music, we were swaying to the melody of their growls and snarls . . . (while my knocking knees served as the rhythm section).

I stole a look over my shoulder and saw the cliff with the river below. I figured I had two choices:

1. Stick around as their dinner guest.
2. Leap off the cliff and practice my skydiving . . . (This time without a parachute.)

Decisions, decisions. To die or to die, that was the question.

(I just wished there were more answers.)

Anyway, after taking a vote of all parties concerned (me, me, and me), the decision was unanimous, the me's had it. I would die—but not by the teeth of these crazy canines with the bad overbites. No sir, I'd check out of this old world by doing what I do best . . . destroying myself through my own God-given clumsiness.

So with a deep breath and another prayer to check if God had changed His mind about those clean clothes, I spun around and raced for the cliff. Of course, my puppy pals were right on my heels . . . literally:

CHOMP!!
"YEOWWWWWWW!"

Unfortunately, the cliff wasn't exactly a cliff. It was more like a steep hill—a very steep hill. Which would explain my

*roll, roll, roll*ing
*tumble, tumble, tumbl*ing,

along with my ever-popular

*bounce, bounce, bounc*ing.

And just when things were getting a little boring (and a lot painful), the hill flattened out a moment. Of course, the drooling doggies were still attached to my behind until I finally

*K-Slamm*ed

into a giant

"OINK!"

pig.

Well, not exactly a pig. Its hairy body, ugly warts, and giant fangs (which begged for the same dental work the dogs needed), not to mention its grumpy personality, told me it was definitely not planning to wind up as anybody's ham dinner.

At least not mine.

At least not my poodle pals.

Instead, the thing gave a few angry grunts followed by a fierce

"SQUEAL!"

Now, unable to speak Pig-ese, I wasn't exactly sure what he meant. But apparently my doggie dudes knew. They immediately let go of my heels (and other parts of my backside) and looked pretty frightened.

The warty warrior grunted a few more times, pawed the earth to show his sincerity . . . and charged at them like a bull. He didn't take a lot of steps, but enough to make the clueless canines turn tail and run, yelping all the way.

Whew, talk about grateful.

Talk about wanting to thank him.

Talk about—uh-oh . . .

Now my hog hero had turned around and was glaring at me. Apparently, I was next on his attack list.

Having no idea what to do, I looked back at the hill. It dropped sharply toward the river. I would have no trouble continuing my rolling, tumbling, and bouncing routine the rest of the way into the water. But I figured I'd already met my quota of broken bones for one story. So, once again, I tried turning the ol' McDoogle charm on this fellow. I cranked up my best smile (which looked more horrified than happy) and after three or four tries finally managed to croak out, "Nice piggy, piggy, piggy . . ."

Now, to be fair, I really don't think he was rude. He probably just didn't hear. I mean, how could he hear anything the way he was pawing the earth, grunting in rage, and squealing as he charged?

SQUEALING AS HE CHARGED?!

Suddenly, *rolling, tumbling, and bouncing* seemed like a great plan—especially for someone with my experience.

So, without a moment's hesitation, I turned and ran for your life. (It would have been for "my" life, but at the moment mine wasn't worth much.)

And I wasn't wrong. Because with every roll, tumble, and bounce, I felt my market value dropping. By the time I reached the water with my ever-popular Wally McDoogle patent-pending

K-Splash,

I was worth about ten cents, if you count the ten-cent deposit for my body. Or zero cents, if you realized that I had just surfaced next to a baby elephant.

Baboons, hyenas, warthogs, baby elephants? What was I, the Crocodile Hunter?

The best I figured, Li'l Dumbo was only a few months old. And he was more than a little cute. Especially the way he tilted his head and looked at me. But that was nothing compared to the way he lowered his trunk, took a snout full of water, and

SPLISSSSHed . . .

it all into my face.

"Hey!" I shouted (in between coughing and drowning). "What do you *cough-cough* think you're *drown-drown* doing?"

He hooted in delight, dipped his built-in fire hose back into the water, and

SPLISSSSHed . . .

me all over again. (Kids nowadays, I tell you, they have no respect for their elders.)

But two could play that game. I leaned back and splashed a huge handful of water into his face. He hooted in joy and sucked up another snout full of water.

This time I saw it coming. I took a deep breath of air and ducked under the surface of the river. No way could he get me there . . . until I felt his trunk slipping under my shirt and tickling my belly.

"Come on, little fellow!" I said, giggling. "Cut it out, now!"

At least that's what I wanted to say. Unfortunately, it came out more like . . . "Blub-blub-blub, glug-blub-glug-blub!" (Hey, you try talking underwater.)

But even that was pretty fun. What wasn't fun was when I started laughing. Actually, that was fun, too. It was the breathing that got a little complicated. The breathing that sounded a lot like . . . "Gag-gag-gag, choke-gag-choke-gag!" (Hey, you try breathing underwater.)

When I finally surfaced, I gasped for air, only to be met again with another

SPLISSSSH.

But it was all in good fun . . . except for the other elephant trunk wrapping around me.

Wait a minute, how many trunks do elephants have?

I opened my eyes in the splashing water. There was Little Dumbo spouting away, having the time of his life. But someone had joined us. Someone about ten times bigger and ten times less happy. Before I could move, the bigger one (I'm betting it was Junior's mommy) tightened her trunk around me and lifted me out of the water.

"Easy, girl!" I shouted. At least that's what I wanted to shout. Unfortunately, it came out more like: "Augh! Augh! I'm going to die! I'm going to die!" (Hey, you try being a coward.)

But Momma wasn't quite done teaching her lesson. To further encourage her baby not to play with strangers (and strangers not to play with her baby), she raised me high over her head—which, of course, led to the necessary and even louder "AUGHHH"*ing* in terror.

Now, I really don't want to complain. I mean, the view up there was actually pretty good. Unfortunately, the ride was a bit bumpy. Especially the part where she suddenly flung me through the air:

"AUGHHHH!"

and I suddenlier

*K-rash*ed

into a tree on the riverbank.

The good news was, I didn't pass out.

The bad news was, well, I didn't pass out. Because by the looks of things, Momma wasn't quite done making her point. As I staggered around, trying to remember how to use my feet, she charged toward me, making it clear that she remembered how to use her tusks.

I stared, frozen in fear. I was trapped with nowhere to run. And then, when she was less than ten feet away, when I was about to become the world's first elephant-kabob, I heard a boy scream.

I looked around, surprised that it wasn't me. In a flash, I was tackled hard from the side, landing on the shore of the river.

Of course, I was dying to know who hit me (and would probably die finding out). But when we landed, I got very involved in

*K-thunk*ing

my head against a very *un*soft rock.

Well, I wish it had been a very unsoft rock.

But by its leathery scales, its lizardlike feet, and giant, snapping crocodile jaws . . . I figured it just might be something like, oh, I don't know . . .

A GIANT SNAPPING CROCODILE!

Ever have one of those days?

It looked like I was about to die one of those deaths. . . .

Chapter 5
The Kid

I rolled onto my belly, raised my head, and looked directly into the mouth of a giant crocodile. And how did I know it was the mouth of a giant crocodile? Believe me, after *My Life As Crocodile Junk Food,* I know all about the mouths of giant crocodiles.

Now, looking inside its mouth wouldn't have been a problem, if I happened to be a crocodile dentist and it happened to be in for its six-month checkup. (Or if I happened to have a rifle, and it was looking to be made into a pair of crocodile-skin boots.) But since I left my drills (and rifle) at home, and since it didn't appear to have an appointment, things got a little interesting.

First, the croc had this thing for my head . . .

It wanted to bite it off!

I was flattered, but I really wanted to save face (along with my ears, hair, and everything

45

else attached to it), so I rolled away as fast as possible.

Next, the croc wanted a free handout (or my hand in its mouth).

I yanked it away, too.

Well, most of it. I was a little slow in the pinky-removal department. But just as its jaws were coming down for some finger food, the little kid who had tackled me suddenly reappeared. He threw his arms around the croc's mouth, slammed it shut, and flipped it onto its back.

Talk about impressive! I mean, the boy was a lot younger than me and a whole lot skinnier (if that's possible), but he easily handled the croc critter.

Once he had it on its back, he shouted something to me. I didn't understand, until he motioned to a nearby dugout canoe close to the riverbank's edge and shouted again.

Now, I'm no genius, but I figured being alive and safe in a canoe was a lot smarter than being dead and in the mouth of a croc. So I scrambled to my feet and raced through the sand to the canoe.

I'd barely jumped inside when I heard the kid running behind me. I spun around just in time to see him grab the side of the boat and shove it toward the water.

The croc—that now seemed even crankier—raced right behind him not twelve feet away.

Better make that ten.

Er, eight.

The kid shouted, obviously wanting me to get out and push. I would have, if my knees hadn't suddenly turned coward on me. I don't want to say they were knocking, but they shook worse than a pair of maracas in a mariachi marching band (whatever that means).

Unable to move, I did the next-best thing. I opened my mouth and:

"AUGHHHHHHH!"*ed.*

(We all have special abilities. For some it's fighting crocodiles, for others it's screaming like a little girl.)

I glanced behind us. The crotchety croc was four feet away and opening its mouth.

We slipped into the water with the canoe.

So did the croc. Now it was two feet away.

Er, one.

The kid leaped into the canoe just as the croc's jaws came down and

K-BIT

into the canoe.

The good news is, dugout canoes are not as

tasty as humans. The bad news is, the croc would have an ugly bruise on its snout—which isn't so bad unless they were having class pictures taken tomorrow.

I started to thank the little kid, but he'd already moved to the front of the canoe, grabbed a makeshift oar, and started to paddle.

I picked up the other oar and tried to help. Unfortunately, no matter how hard I paddled, it was always in the wrong direction. And after ten minutes of sending us into little figure-eight circles, one way, then the other way, then the other way again, I figured I'd be more helpful if I stopped.

Of course, I had a thousand and one questions to ask the kid. Intelligent things like . . .

—What do people call him when they don't call him "kid"?
—Where were we going?
—Was he taking me to his village to eat me?

But since we couldn't communicate, I decided to wait.

The sun had finally come up, and I could see all sorts of cool trees and stuff along the bank. The whole place was like a jungle but a lot drier. And hotter. In no time flat, the kid had his old ragged T-shirt peeled off. Now he sat on his knees paddling, sweat pouring off his back, wearing only a pair of ugly worn gym shorts and some goofy-looking sandals that had soles made of old tires. I didn't want to say anything about his wardrobe, but the guy was definitely fashion-impaired.

I felt bad that he was doing all the work, so I decided to paddle again. He heard me reach for the oar and spun around. He jabbered something I didn't understand, until his teeth flashed in a bright white smile. Only then did I realize he was making a joke about my seafaring skills. He jabbered some more, grinned some more, then grabbed my oar and threw it into the water out of my reach.

I had to laugh. It was nice to know that despite the culture gap, we could still communicate through the international language of my clumsiness.

After a few minutes, I laid my head back in the warm sun and closed my eyes. Only then did I think about my superhero story. And with nothing else to do, I started imagining what would happen next to Rhyming Dude McDoogle. . . .

When we last left our hero, he was being transported to Material Man's

headquarters in Hollyweird by the awful...

Ta-da-DAAAA...

Give-Me-It-All Beam.

For the most part, it was an okay trip...except for the in-flight movie, which he'd already seen, and the two-and-a-half microsized pretzels they gave him for a snack. (I guess even transport beams are trying to cut down on expenses.)

Then there was the minor cross-wiring problem. Apparently, Material Man had also discovered a Four-H prizewinning hog that he wanted. And since he beamed in the hog and Rhyming Dude at about the same time, their body parts got a little confused. No biggie, except that Rhyming Dude hated his new curly tail and wasn't really fond of having four legs. Of course he complained, but it came out like:

*"Oinky, oink-oink,
Oink, oink, oinky-oink!"*

The good news was, he was still talking in rhyme. The bad news was, nobody could understand him. (Then again, with his incredible lack of talent, maybe that wasn't such bad news after all.)

"SQUEAL!"

Sorry. (Guess he still understands English.)

"Not only that," Material Man interrupts, "but a pig?"

"What's wrong with a pig?" I asked.

"Isn't that a little too close to real life?"

"What do you mean?"

"I mean, didn't you just escape from a real live warthog?"

"That was a crocodile."

"No, in the chapter before that."

"Oinky,
Oink-oink.
Oink!"

Apparently, our hog hero agreed.

"So what do you suggest?" I asked.

*"Squealy,
Squeal, squeal."*

Material Man nods. **"Perfect."**

"What did he say?"

"It's your imagination, don't you know?"

"It's been a long day."

"He said it would make more sense if he became mixed up with his big-screen TV."

"Big-screen TV?"

"Yeah, the one I was beaming over at the very beginning of the story."

"Oh, right, of course." (It *has* been a long day.)

"Well?"

"Well, what?"

"Can we get back to our story?"

"Oh, right. Sorry."

In a flash, Material Man reverses the Give-Me-It-All Beam

BOP BEEP

and our hero returns with his body stuck inside a giant-screen TV. Which isn't bad, except every time he talks

he sounds like one of those used-car commercials....

"Come on down
To Rhyming Dude's car lot.
Buy my junky cars,
Which keep falling apart a lot!"

Fortunately, rhyming superheroes can't lie.
Unfortunately, being on TV doesn't improve their rhyming.

"Hey, I heard that!"

"Sorry."

"Now, get me out of this TV,
Let's get on with the show.
If you won't buy a used car,
Then help me vanquish my foe."

I nodded and thought harder, until I was back into the story:

Once again, our vicious villain re-beams Rhyming Dude until he appears in the Hollyweird hideout exactly like he's supposed to (except for the 120 channels he can get for just $29.95 a month by plugging a cable into the back of his—)

"Ahem." Rhyming Dude "Ahem"ed.

I frowned and thought harder:

At last, our hero arrives in Material Man's lair. The showdown is just about to begin, when suddenly—

"Shhh—"
What is it now?
But this time it wasn't Rhyming Dude or Material Man interrupting my story. It was the little kid.

I opened my eyes to see that he had quit paddling. He was looking over his shoulder and staring inside the canoe next to my leg. I looked down to see that a snake had crawled out of the river and joined me. I opened my mouth, preparing to scream my lungs out, when the kid shook his head. He raised his fingers to his lips and motioned for me to be perfectly still.

Of course, this was the last thing I wanted to

do, but he seemed pretty serious so I stayed frozen (except for the part where my whole body shook in terror).

I watched as the snake raised its head onto my lap, its tongue flickering back and forth. Slowly, it slithered over me.

Now, the way I looked at it, I figured I had four choices:

1. Pass out in fear.
2. Wet my pants.
3. Run to Mommy.
4. All of the above.

Fortunately, the kid didn't give me time to do any of them. Instead, he took his paddle in both hands and slowly turned around in the canoe.

I looked on, my heart pounding faster than a jackhammer on too much caffeine.

The snake had stretched across one of my legs, then down into the canoe between them, and was slithering over my other leg.

The kid slowly raised the paddle over his head.

I looked up, wondering which would hurt worse . . . being clobbered by a paddle or swallowed by a snake.

Then in one swift

WHISSHHHH
K-Thud!

the kid slammed the paddle down between my legs. He cut the snake completely in half, but that didn't stop it from screaming:

"AUGHHHHH!"

And screaming some more:

"AUGH! AUGH! AUGH! AUGH!"

For a moment, I didn't think it would ever stop . . . until I realized it wasn't the snake screaming, but me. (Some habits really are hard to break.) I immediately closed my mouth, and immediately the screaming ended. (What a coincidence.)

I leaped to my feet, trying to brush the snake parts off me. It wasn't a bad idea, except for the part of standing up in a canoe. Actually, it wasn't the standing that was bad, it was the

"Whoa, Waa, Wooo . . ."

part of me trying to keep my balance and, of course, losing it with an

"AUGH!"
K-Splash!

dip into the murky water.

Actually, the dip was kind of refreshing. It was the embarrassment that happened when I came up for air. The embarrassment of a dozen old people standing on the riverbank laughing at, who else but . . .

Me.

Chapter 6

A Not-So-Super Supper

After a few minutes of splashing around, doing my usual drowning routine, one of the old-timers on the riverbank waded in and pulled me out. Of course, I dropped to my knees and coughed up a couple of gallons of water (not to mention a lung or two).

When I finally staggered to my feet, I saw about a dozen people standing around me. They were mostly old men and women with a few children. Their skinny bodies were a lot like the kids', and their ragged clothing made it clear they all shopped at the same store (or waste disposal site).

Once they saw I was all right, everyone began grinning, slapping me on the back, and teasing me. (I guess if they were going to eat me, they wanted to make sure I'd be a "Happy Meal.")

The little kid pulled the canoe up on the beach and we all started toward a small group of huts. They weren't much to look at, just round buildings with mud walls and straw roofs. As far as I could tell, there was no electricity; no running water; and, horror of horrors, no Internet.

But if they were suffering you couldn't tell it, not by their beaming faces. I don't want to say they were happy, but if they shone any brighter you'd need sunglasses to look at them.

As we approached the village, an old-timer limped out of a hut to greet me. He had the same tattered clothes as everyone else, but he wore a golfer's hat. The best I figured, he was like the chief or something. So, putting on my best manners, I slowed to a stop and spoke:

"ME . . . WALLY!" I pounded my chest. "ME VERY HAPPY TO MEET YOU!" (Why do we think yelling helps people understand us?)

He looked at me quizzically. It was obvious I wasn't getting through, so I tried again:

"ME TASTY TASTE VERY BAD!" I pretended to bite my arm and spit. "ICKY, ICKY! ME NO GOOD FOR DINNER!"

He flashed a grin that was missing more than a few teeth and answered, "That's cool, dude. I don't like white meat anyway."

If my jaw had dropped any lower, it would have been dragging on the ground.

"You speak . . . English?" I asked.

"So do you."

"But . . . where . . . how?"

"It's kinda necessary in order to graduate from college."

"You went to college?"

"Bible college, yeah. A long time ago."

"But how—"

"A mission group paid for it," he said. "What about you?"

"I'm not old enough for college."

He chuckled. "No, I mean, how'd you get here?" He motioned to the kid who'd canoed me. "Tomba says you dropped out of the sky."

Catching on, I nodded. "Oh yeah. Kinda. We were having some airplane trouble, and I kinda accidentally hit the wrong lever and kinda accidentally parachuted out of the plane."

"Those are some incredible accidents."

"Not if you know my incredible world."

"What about the others? Is everybody else all right?"

I shrugged. "Now that I've left them, I'm sure they're a lot safer."

"We better get on the shortwave radio and let your parents know you're okay. By the way," he said, reaching out his hand, "I'm Benbawozonbwa."

"Ben-who-whaza?"

He laughed. "No, Benbawozonbwa."

I was about to try again. But realizing I'd probably sprain my mouth, he chuckled. "Just call me Ben. And you are?"

"Wally. Wally McDoogle."

An old village woman rushed toward us, all excited. She was jabbering a mile a minute and getting the other folks all worked up.

"What is it?" I asked. "What's going on?"

"Sounds like we've found some dinner."

"What?"

"Come on."

We followed the group past the huts and along a red clay path that led deeper and deeper into the jungle.

"They're this excited about dinner?" I asked.

He nodded. "We haven't eaten since yesterday."

"You're kidding!"

He shook his head. "The government has taken all our young men. The rest of us are either too old or too feeble to hunt."

I looked around. "But everybody is so . . . so . . ."

"So what?"

"So happy."

"Why shouldn't we be?"

"A day without eating," I said. "I get cranky missing *one* meal."

He gave a toothless grin. "These people have something more than food to make them happy."

I was about to ask him what, when we turned off the path and made our way through thicker brush. Well, everybody else made their way through thicker brush. I was a little too busy

"AUGH!"

falling into a hidden hole.

The good news was, I only broke a minimal amount of bones. The bad news was, everybody crowded around the hole and looked down at me like I was the village idiot . . . (which is okay 'cause everybody needs to be known for something).

Ben stooped and groaned as his old joints cracked and popped. He dropped onto his stomach and reached down to help me out.

"Sorry about that," he said. "It's an old trap we set when there were lions in the area."

I grabbed his hand and he started to pull me up, until I slipped and fell.

Not once, not twice, but the usual McDoogle dozens of times.

When I finally got out and we'd started through the brush again, I said, "You said these people had something more than food to make them happy."

"That's right."

"Like what?"

"Like God."

"What does that mean?"

"It means their friendship with God is where they get their joy—not in what they eat or drink." With a twinkle in his eyes, he added, "Or who is trying to drown themselves in our river or fall into our lion traps."

I nodded. "That's pretty cool. I believe in God, too."

"Then you know what I'm talking about."

I started to answer, but realized I couldn't. I mean, just a day ago I was grumbling 'cause there weren't any presents under the tree. But these people, I mean—they had nothing, and they were still happy. I glanced down at my fancy cargo pants and my $150 tennis shoes, suddenly feeling a bit uncomfortable.

A few moments later we came into an open field where there were a dozen mounds of red dirt piled six to eight feet high. The villagers cried out in excitement and raced to the mounds. Then, ever so carefully, they started digging away at them.

"What are those?" I asked.

"Termite hills," Ben explained. "We're digging into them to find the termites, especially the queens."

"Why?"

"That's what we came for." He motioned to one of the men who had just pulled something out and was carefully laying it on a large leaf. Ben called for him to approach. As he did, I saw it was a giant insect. It had a tiny head and tiny feet. But the bottom half of its body was almost half a foot long and two, maybe three inches wide. Talk about freaky looking.

"What is that?" I asked.

"A queen termite." He glanced at the other hills. "By the looks of things, we'll be able to get quite a few of them before dinner."

I frowned. "What do termites have to do with dinner?"

He looked at me and grinned. "They *are* dinner."

* * * * *

The night's feast was not exactly the type of Christmas meal I'd dreamed of having.

The good news was, there was no wild dancing, crazy jumping, or spear throwing. (It's hard to have wild dancing, crazy jumping, and spear throwing when everyone's a thousand years old and weak from hunger.) The bad news was, there were plenty of termites to go around.

And since I was the special guest of honor . . .

"Please," Ben said. He offered me the fat, squishy critter still bubbling in its juices from the fire he'd just taken it out of.

"No, that's okay," I said, swallowing back my queasy stomach that had its own bubbling juices.

"No," he insisted, "you must go first. Please, take as much as you want."

I didn't have the heart to tell him I was already taking as much as I wanted (zero). I glanced up at the villagers. Their old wrinkled faces were staring at me, grinning, happy to share.

"You're the guest," Ben explained. "They won't start until you do."

Great. If I didn't eat, they wouldn't eat. And by the looks of their skinny bodies, the quicker they started, the better.

Ben tried to encourage me. "If you like crunchy, go for the head and feet—just don't let the little antennas get caught between your teeth. But if you like chewy, you'll really enjoy the belly with all the eggs."

Somehow, my appetite didn't improve. I looked up at him, hopelessly.

He nodded at me, encouragingly.

I looked at my dinner hosts, helplessly.

They nodded at me, eagerly.

There was no way out. So, with nothing to lose except whatever was left in my stomach, I pointed to the head.

In one swift move, Ben cut it off, scraped it onto my leaf plate, and motioned for me to eat.

In one shaky move, I raised it to my lips.

Suddenly, I remembered to say grace. I closed my eyes and silently prayed, *Dear Lord, please don't let this kill me.* Then, opening one eye and peering down at the delicacy, I added, *And if You want me to die beforehand, that would be okay, too—with or without the clean clothes.*

I opened my eyes, took a deep breath, and popped it into my mouth.

Everybody grinned and dug in.

I was happy to see them eating. (I would have been happier if I could eat, too.) Actually, I did manage to keep down the head, and even tried the feet. I'd like to say it tasted just like chicken. (I'd like to say that, but I can't.) Instead it tasted and crunched more like . . . well, more like roasted termite head and feet (except for the antennas, which got caught between my teeth).

But the taste and crunch were nothing compared to the swallowing. I'm not positive, but I thought for sure that I felt a foot or two trying to crawl back up my throat.

Then came the entertainment . . . (as if trying to swallow wasn't entertainment enough). It really wasn't much, just the old people quietly humming and singing different songs as they ate. But it really sounded cool.

I leaned over to Ben and asked, "What are they singing? What are the words?"

He smiled. "Hymns."

"Hymns?" I frowned.

He nodded. "They're thanking God."

"For this?"

"Of course."

My frown grew deeper.

"What's wrong?"

"It's just . . . I mean, if this is the best God has to offer, I wouldn't exactly be thanking Him."

"Why not?"

I paused to swallow back another escaping leg. When I finished, I explained. "Why would they thank God for putting them in the middle of a famine where this is all they get to eat?"

It was Ben's turn to look puzzled.

I continued. "I was talking to this guy on our flight over here. He said that a thousand people die in our world from hunger every hour."

Ben nodded. "That sounds about right."

"So how can they thank a God who is causing that to happen?" I could feel myself getting a little hot under the collar. "How can they tell God, 'Thank You for—'"

"Whoa, whoa, whoa." Ben held up his hands. "You think all those starving people are God's fault?"

"Who else's fault could it be?"

"Man's."

"What?"

"It's not God's fault they're starving. It's man's fault."

I shook my head. "It's not man's fault there isn't enough food in the world to eat."

"Who said anything about there not being enough food?"

I frowned even harder. "Why else would a thousand people die every hour?"

"Greed."

"What?"

"Man's greed."

If my frown had gotten any deeper, it would have popped out the back of my head.

Ben saw it and explained. "Each day the world produces four and a half pounds of food for every man, woman, and child on earth."

"Four and a half pounds?"

"That's right. And that's more than enough to feed every single person in the world every single day."

"Then how come"—I pointed to the villagers—"I mean, why don't they—"

"Why don't they have enough food?" he asked.

I nodded.

"Because people are too stingy to ship it to them."

"What??"

"Oh yeah." I could see it was Ben's turn to get a little steamed. "We have more than enough money and food to feed every single person in the world every single day. We just don't want to. *Man* doesn't want to. He'd rather spend it on his fancy homes or cars or TV sets or clothes."

I could only stare at him.

"No, Wally," he said, shaking his head, "it's not God's fault people are starving to death. It's man's. It's his greed. It's because he's always wanting to buy bigger and better stuff, while people like these"—he motioned around him—"are literally starving to death."

I looked around the campfire, suddenly losing what little appetite I had. I glanced down at my fancy tennis shoes flickering in the firelight. My $150 shoes that I had thrown a fit for Mom to buy me just a couple of weeks earlier; $150 that could have bought some of these very same people something to eat . . .

Chapter 7

Sleep Tight,
Don't Let the Bedbugs
(OR TARANTULAS!) Bite

Ben had trouble getting the shortwave radio to
work. He could receive but not broadcast—something about the batteries being too low. Then he
told me worse news.

"Wally, you won't be safe here much longer."

"Why?" I asked.

"The militia will come for you."

"The what?"

"It's sort of like an army."

"That's great! They'll help me find my family," I said.

"No, Wally, that's bad. The militia doesn't
like foreigners, especially Americans. They may
try to capture you—or worse."

"But how would they know I'm here?"

"They probably saw your parachute."

I looked around at the smiling faces. "What
about all of you?" I asked.

Ben shrugged. "Unfortunately, it's all too common for the militia to raid our village. But we know how to escape, and survive."

* * * * *

We decided I should spend the night at Tomba's place. Early the next morning Tomba would lead me to the city. It would be a long day of traveling, so Ben suggested I go to bed early.

It sounded good to me. After parachuting out of an airplane; wrestling with more wildlife than a zookeeper; eating strange, exotic food (well, at least strange); and feeling lousy about owning such fancy shoes, I figured hitting Tomba's bedroom and grabbing some sleep would be a great idea.

The only problem was, Tomba had no bedroom . . . or bed. Come to think of it, there wasn't much sleep, either.

For starters, all of Tomba's family stayed in the same room—which also served as the living room, family room, kitchen, and dining room (fortunately, the bathroom was outside). And when I say *all* of his family, I mean *all* of his four little brothers and sisters, his mom, oh, and let's not forget Grandma (who snored so loudly I thought they'd built a racetrack around the hut . . . for semitrucks).

Then there was the matter of the beds . . . or lack of them. We all slept on grass mats on a dirt floor. Actually, the dirt floor wasn't bad since Momma Tomba had it swept cleaner than any home I've ever visited. Seriously, it may have been dirt, but it was so clean you could have eaten off it . . . which, of course, you couldn't since there was nothing to eat.

I fell asleep pretty fast, but a few hours later I awoke to the sound of

SNOOOOORK . . .

Grandma

WHEEEEZE . . .

snoring away.

I tried to go back to sleep, but there were just too many things racing around inside my brain . . . and around the room. You could barely hear them, but there was definitely something in there. I mean, there was no missing the faint

nibble, nibble, crunch, crunch

of some critter munching away.

The good news was, it was not munching on any of my fingers, toes, or nose. As far as I could tell, everything was intact. I figured it was probably just one of those termite guys who had decided to grab a bite to eat (like a nearby table leg or something) while he was in the vicinity.

Whatever it was, after a while the gentle, rhythmic sound helped me relax. I mean, between that and Grandma's snoring

SNOOOOORK . . .
nibble, nibble, crunch, crunch
WHEEEEZE . . .

I was almost being lulled back to sleep.

Almost.

Unfortunately, a new distraction began. I felt it move across my arm, then onto my chest. My eyes popped open and then bugged out like Ping-Pong balls. Because there, slowly making its way across my chest, was, you guessed it, a tarantula!

I tried to shout, I tried to scream, but it's hard to do either when you're too scared to breathe. So the only noise filling the hut was your standard, everyday

SNOOOOORK . . .
nibble, nibble, crunch, crunch
WHEEEEZE . . .

Using all of my will power, I slowly moved my free hand toward Tomba, who was sleeping beside me.

SNOOOOORK . . .
nibble, nibble, crunch, crunch

I gave him a poke in the ribs. He didn't move.

WHEEEEZE . . .
nibble, nibble, crunch, crunch

I poked harder.
More in the nothing department.

SNOOOOORK . . .
nibble, nibble, crunch, crunch

Now the thing turned and started moving up my chest toward my face.

WHEEEEZE . . .
nibble, nibble, crunch, crunch

I dug my fingers so hard into Tomba's ribs that I felt like I was doing open-heart surgery!

The good news was, it woke him up.

The bad news was, when he turned to look at me he started to giggle.

I wanted to join in, but I didn't see a lot of humor in having a stare-down with a tarantula.

The hairy thing continued moving up my chest until it was about seven inches from my mouth. I wasn't sure whether to pass out from fear or just have a heart attack and be done with it.

Tomba saved me the trouble. He reached for his sandal. Then, in one quick move, he brushed off the spider and smashed it onto the dirt floor with a sickening

SQUISH-CRUNCH.

Before I could start breathing again, let alone have a good nervous breakdown, he looked at me and started laughing.

I frowned. "What's so funny?"

He pointed to my hair and kept laughing.

I reached up to touch it. Well, I tried to touch it. But for some reason it was a lot shorter than I remembered. In fact, there seemed to be huge tufts of it missing.

He laughed even harder.

"What?" I demanded. "What's so funny? What happened to my hair?"

He spotted something on the ground beside me and quickly scooped it up. Opening his palm, he showed me a large cockroach. It didn't appear to be concerned about being captured. Instead, it sat very calmly in his hand, nibbling away. Nibbling away on something that could only be . . . a lock of my hair!

* * * * *

After an hour or two (or five), things started settling down . . . a little—until we were awakened by the sound of either firecrackers or a backfiring car. At least that's what I thought it was . . . until Ben came bursting into the hut with another option:

"It's the militia!"

In seconds everyone was up on their feet, running around, crying out, and trying to wake

SNORK-OORK-ORK . . .
WHEEEEZE . . . cough, cough

Grandma.

I'd barely had time to reach over and grab

my glasses (which I was grateful to see were not on the cockroach's menu) before Ben was pulling me to my feet.

The fireworks or whatever they were sounded a lot closer.

"You must leave at once!" Ben shouted. "Tomba will take you into the bush! Hurry!"

Before I knew it, Tomba took my other hand and was dragging me toward the open door.

Outside there was a lot of commotion and bright lights.

I stumbled into one side of the doorway

"OAFF!"

then turned and ran into the other side.

"OAFF! OAFF!"

"Wally!"

I spun back to Ben.

"Put on your glasses."

I nodded (no wonder he was the chief). I slipped them on just in time to see

WHOOOSH . . .

the hut across the way suddenly catch fire. Beside

it stood two or three men in uniforms. They were laughing and shouting. Beside them was an army-type truck with a giant gun in the back.

"What are they doing?" I cried. "What's going on?"

"They are looking for you. Now go!!"

Ben nodded to Tomba, who yanked me through the door and outside. Immediately, we crouched down and started to run, doing our best to stay out of sight.

After five or six steps, I realized that I'd

"Ouch! Ouch!"
"Ooooch, ooooch, ouch!"

forgotten my shoes.

I wanted to go back and get them but had second thoughts. Call me chicken, but there was something about all the commotion and people running this way and that. Then there was the screaming—women, children, old men . . . the very folks who were so quietly singing hymns earlier that night. Finally, of course, there were the fireworks. Not the Fourth of July kind, but the kind made by soldiers firing guns.

Tomba continued pulling me to the other side of the camp where we ducked behind one of the huts and then made our way into the bush.

We ran along a path that Tomba must have known was there because I didn't see a thing— just darkness, bushes, and an occasional tree branch

*K-Slapp*ing

me in the face.

I heard plenty more screaming and another

WHOOSH

as someone else's hut was being set afire.

The village homes were being destroyed because of *me*!

Tomba was risking his life to protect *me*!

I tried to stop, to turn around and go back. But Tomba would have none of it. Instead, he pulled harder.

A flashlight beam flared in our direction. Tomba jerked me down into the brush. I started to complain, but he motioned for me to be silent . . . and for good reason.

The beam swept past as two soldiers raced down the path we'd taken.

We held our breath and stayed low until they passed us and were gone.

The screaming back at the village grew louder.

Again, I wanted to head back. But again, Tomba would not listen. Instead, he rose to make sure all was clear. When he was certain, he helped me to my feet, and we started running another direction in the dark.

Another direction that followed no path.

Another direction that had even more

K-slap, K-slap, K-slap

tree branches, which also explained the additional number of

K-Thud
"Oaff!"

tree trunks.

And don't even get me started on the extra

"Ouch! Ouch!"
"Ooooch, ooooch, ouch!"

from whatever my bare tootsies were treading on.

Chapter 8

A Midnight Swim

I didn't know which hurt more . . . my heart for what was happening to all those people back at the village, or my bare feet for stepping on every thorn, sharp twig, and jagged rock in Africa.

(I suspected it was my heart, though you wouldn't know it by all the

> "Ouch! Ouch!"
> "Ooooch, ooooch, ouch"*es*

I was screaming during our little run.)

Unfortunately, screaming is not the best way to make a silent escape. In no time flat, those two pesky owners of that pesky flashlight heard me and doubled back after us.

Of course, they were doing a lot of shouting and yelling. But despite their *sweet-talking* death threats, neither Tomba nor I felt like stopping and giving them the time of day (or night).

Instead, we ran harder through the bush until we suddenly veered off to the left. In just a few moments we found the

K-Splash

river.

Of course, my swimming skills hadn't exactly improved over the past twenty-four hours. But I guess mine were a lot better than the bad guys'. Because instead of leaping in after us, they stopped at the bank and refused to come in.

Ha! I thought. *We beat them!* When it came to swimming, those big, bad bullies were nothing but cowardly chickens. Of course, so was I, but at least I was going to be a drowned cowardly chicken. I frowned. Suddenly, I was not so sure if I liked that idea.

I frowned even harder when the bad boys turned from the river and ran back into the bush for all they were worth.

I wanted to ask Tomba what was going on, but at the moment I was too busy sinking to the bottom of the river. Well . . . I should have been sinking to the bottom of the river, but for some reason the bottom of the river was coming up to me.

Soon it touched my bruised and battered feet with its soft, spongy tongue. Talk about luxury. No thorns, no sharp twigs, no jagged rocks. Just a soft, spongy tongue and giant, pearly molars.

SOFT, SPONGY TONGUE AND GIANT, PEARLY MOLARS!!

(sorry)

Where am I? What's going on?!
(Don't worry, I really don't expect you to have the answers, but if you have any clues, feel free to drop me an e-mail.)

Tomba gave me no answers, either. But by the looks of things, he had a solution. Unfortunately, the solution involved throwing his arm around my neck, choking me to death, and yanking me out of the hippopotamus's mouth.

HIPPOPOTAMUS'S MOUTH!!?

(Forget the e-mail, I think I've got it figured out.)

Of course, the hippo was not about to let us leave without a few parting gifts—(missing arms, legs, heads, that kind of thing). So she snapped her jaws shut with a ferocious

K-CHOMP!

The good news was, Tomba pulled me away just in time.

The bad news was, she was not done with her hippo high jinks.

She came after us again, opening her mouth. Tomba spotted a nearby log and dragged it toward us. Then, just as those pearly whites surrounded us, coming down for an encore performance, my little buddy shoved the log between her teeth. She hit it with more than your average, run-of-the-mill

K-CRUNCH!

Lucky for us, enjoying her new dietary supplement gave us time to scramble out of the way. Unlucky for hippo girl, she got more fiber in her diet than she bargained for . . . plus several dozen gumpicks (they'd have been toothpicks, but these splinters sank deep into her lips and, you guessed it, gums).

She let out a roar of anger (almost as bad as when Dad can't find the TV remote) and then started to

Hic-Hic-Hiccup.

Poor thing. I wanted to stick around and tell her to try holding her breath, or at least have someone give her a good scare—but Tomba thought it would be better if we swam as fast as we could toward the bank.

I agreed.

Once we got there, I dropped to my knees, figuring this was as good a place as any to have a heart attack. But Tomba helped me to my feet, and we started running. Actually, he did most of the running. I was in charge of the dragging of feet and falling to the ground. (Hey, we all have our specialties.)

Finally, neither Tomba nor I could take another step. We were far enough away that the hiccupping hippo would not follow. And there was no way the bad guys would risk entering the river to go after us. I mean, who would be stupid enough to swim in a river with hippos?

(Don't answer that.)

So, with nothing else to do but collapse on the ground and rest for a while, we decided to . . . collapse on the ground and rest for a while.

Well, collapse on the ground, anyway.

Unfortunately, my mind wasn't exactly in the mood for resting. So, pretty soon, as often happens, I began thinking of my superhero story . . .

When we last left Rhyming Dude McDoogle, he was saving the West Coast from tilting into the water because of all the stuff Material Man is collecting. Our heroically handsome hero has just been beamed into the bad-deed doer's secret Hollyweird hideout.

Well...maybe not so secret. It's hard to be secret when you're the proud owner of:

—17,524 different types of swimming pools (stacked end on end, which makes for some tricky swimming).

—10,332 supercool cars (even trickier 'cause he's only got a one-car garage).

—And let's not forget all those football stadiums.

Nobody's sure what made Material Man so materialistic....

Some think it was because when he was a baby his mother left him in front of the Buy-All-the-Junk-We're-Selling channel for seventy-two hours nonstop.

Others blame his father for replacing his entire set of Uno cards with MasterCharge cards.

Then there's the ever-popular theory that his brain was miswired so that he thought all news reports were commercials and all commercials were news reports. (Poor guy, he could never figure out why folks would want to buy earthquakes, hurricanes, or traffic jams. But at the same time, he obeyed all the commercials that screamed: "You gotta have this!" "You gotta buy these!" "You'll never be happy without that!")

Whatever his reason, the materialistic maniac has piled up more stuff than Mom buys when she goes to a Saturday morning garage sale. (Well, almost.) And now, our heroically handsome hero searches the hideous hideout for him.

Suddenly, the entire left coast

K-REEEAK...

tilts down several more feet. Our hero cries:

"Material Man!
Stop destroying our land!
Your greedy plan
Has gotten out of ha——"

"No need to shout," Material Man
says, chuckling from behind him.
"Unless it's in excitement over all
this cool stuff I've collected for
you."

Our hero spins around and gasps.
All around Material Man, on every
side, are stacks and stacks of

Ta-da-DAAAA...

books.

But not just any books. No, dear
reader, these are stacks and stacks
of every Dr. Seuss book ever written!

Our hero can barely find his voice.
"They're...they're...beautiful."

Material Man smiles a sinister
smile. "Yes, they are, you impossibly
impoverished poet. And they all can
be yours. All yours."

Rhyming Dude takes a step toward
them, whispering in disbelief:

"All mine?
They're so incredibly fine.
Please, please, tell me
This isn't some line!"

Unable to endure such beauty, our hero slowly sinks to his knees, trembling in awe. As he does, the earth gives another

K-REEEAK...

But Rhyming Dude barely hears. He's too hypnotized by what he sees.

"That's right." The criminally uncool character cackles his characteristically creepy chuckle.

TRANSLATION: The bad guy laughed.

"All you have to do is leave me alone. All you have to do is let me keep collecting my stuff."

Still, despite Rhyming Dude's growing greed for the books, there is some flicker of heroism hiding in his humanity.

TRANSLATION: He hasn't gone completely crackers.

Somehow he is able to answer in a voice faint and very far away:

"What of the land
In your plan that's so ungrand?
What of the children, mothers,
   and fathers
Who soon will be tilting into
   the waters?"

Material Man shudders at the terrible poetry. But pulling himself together, he manages to speak a sneakingly sinister sentence. "That's not your concern, Rhyming Dude."

"It's not?
Tell me, I must have forgot...."

"You'll have all these wonderful books. That's all that counts. Who cares about a few million drowning people?"

Slowly, Rhyming Dude begins to nod.

"Of course,
What was I thinking?

So what if the West Coast
Does all of that sinking."

"That's right." Material Man
motions to the stacks of books. "Stop
fighting me. Let me have my way, and
every one of these books will be
yours...all yours."

Unable to turn his eyes away, our
hero takes a step toward the books.
And then another.

As if protesting, the West Coast

K-REEEAKs...

again, even louder.

But Rhyming Dude does not notice
as he reaches toward the brilliantly
beautiful books.

Unable to contain himself, the
dastardly dangerous dude lets out a
mighty "Moo-hoo-hoo-ha-ha-ha" (the
chuckle legally required by all dastardly dangerous dudes just before
they have their dastardly dude ways).

Oh, no. What will happen next?
Will the West Coast sink into the
ocean never again to be seen? What

will happen to Disneyland, Universal Studios, and Knott's Berry Farm? And is there more to the West Coast than just California? Who knows? Who cares? (Though I bet those people in Washington and Oregon might have some thoughts on the matter.)

But, even more importantly, does this mean there will no longer be any more *Cat in the Hat* books for children to read? Even more importantlier (don't try that word at home, kids), does that mean they'll have to read more *My Life As...* books instead?

(Hmm, I guess every dastardly dark cloud has a silver lining....)

These and other horrifically horrific thoughts haunted my head when I felt Tomba shaking me awake.

I tried to sound intelligent, but no matter what language you speak, "Huh, uh, duh, um . . ." always comes out like, well, like, "Huh, uh, duh, um . . ."

Unfortunately, that was about the most intelligent thing I would be saying (or doing) for a very long while. . . .

Chapter 9

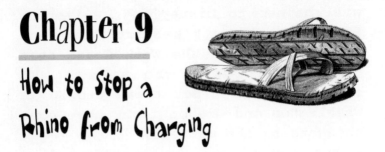

How to Stop a Rhino from Charging

Once Tomba got me awake, he motioned for me to hurry.

"But—" I pointed back to his village. "What about your parents, your friends?"

He shook his head and pointed in the direction of the city.

"Forget it," I said. We have to see if we can help." I turned and started back the way we had come—which was a pretty good idea, except for my first

"AUGH!"
stumble, stumble, FALL

step.

I couldn't believe the pain. It felt like a hundred people were jabbing a hundred needles into my feet. I looked down and saw the reason.

The bottoms of them were covered in more bloody cuts and scrapes than my brother Burt's (or was it Brock's?) face the first time he tried shaving with Dad's safety razor.

Tomba dropped down beside me to take a look. He shook his head, frowning.

"Don't worry about it," I said. "We have to check on your village."

I rose to my feet and took another step. At least that's what I wanted to do. Unfortunately, my feet were more in the mood for an encore

"AUGH!"
stumble, stumble, FALL

performance.

Without a word, Tomba pulled off his own goofy-looking, tire-tread sandals.

"What are you doing?" I asked.

He said nothing as he reached for one of my feet and slipped a sandal on it. It was a little on the tight side, but it mostly fit.

"No way!" I argued. "What are *you* going to wear?"

The little guy gave a grin and slapped the bottom of his foot. It looked almost as tough as the tire tread. But I still wasn't about to take his only shoes.

"No way!" I repeated.

He shook his head and slipped off the second sandal.

"Tomba!?"

He tried putting it on my foot.

I didn't let him. "You can't just give me your shoes. They're the only pair you've got."

But he wouldn't take no for an answer. He just kept grinning bigger and nodding harder, like he wanted to do it. Not only wanted, but like he was actually happy about it!

"Tomba!"

Somehow he grabbed my foot, and though I put up a fight, he managed to slip it on.

"Tomba!!"

Then, without a word, he tugged me to my feet.

"All right, all right," I agreed. "I'll wear them. But just until we get to your village and I can find my own shoes."

With that, I turned and started hobbling back toward his village. My feet still hurt, and to be honest, I was doing a lot more limping than walking, but at least I was getting my way. Or so I thought.

I'd only taken three or four steps when I looked over my shoulder and saw Tomba had not moved.

"Come on," I said, motioning. "We gotta see what happened."

But he shook his head again and pointed the opposite direction toward the city.

"Right," I said, nodding, "but after we check on your village."

The little guy shook his head. Then he pretended to hold a make-believe rifle and shouted, "Boom, boom! Boom, boom!"

"You think the soldiers are still there?"

He nodded yes.

"Then we *have* to help," I argued. "We have to go back and—"

Again, he shook his head and pointed toward the city.

I shook my own head.

"Boom, boom!" he shouted.

"I don't care," I said. "We gotta help!"

Having made up my mind, I turned and headed back for the village. There was just one problem . . . I wasn't sure which direction it was. I thought I knew, but after a half-dozen more steps, I wasn't so sure. I mean, I knew it was near the river, but . . . exactly where was the river? We had run so far last night, I couldn't even hear it.

I turned back to Tomba. The little fellow had folded his arms and refused to move.

Well, two could play that game. I folded my own arms and refused to move.

I'm not sure how long we waited. It could have been a minute; it could have been five. All I know is that there were suddenly a lot more flies buzzing around than I remembered from the day before. And they all had their little fly brains focused on sticking their little fly teeth (do flies have teeth?) into my little human skin.

But it made no difference to me. I didn't care if I was a walking blood bank for every insect in Africa, nothing would make me move.

Well . . . almost nothing.

It started as a little rustle in the bushes off to our left.

No problem; there were lots of rustlings out here. It came with all the little critters.

Next there were the snortings and grunts . . . *big* snortings and grunts.

(So much for *little* critters.)

I swallowed nervously and glanced at Tomba.

He swallowed nervously and looked at the bushes.

Next came the snapping of twigs . . . *big* twigs (as in logs and trees).

I tried swallowing again, but I had run out of stuff to swallow. I looked at Tomba. So had he.

Still neither of us would give up our ground.

Until the ground started shaking! The reason was simple: Granted, I'm no geologist or anything, but have you ever noticed how the ground starts shaking whenever a two-and-a-half-ton rhinoceros comes stampeding out of the brush at you?

No? Well, then I guess you'll just have to take my word for it.

Or Tomba's.

Because we both looked at the charging rhino, then at each other, and in a flash we both had the same, identical thought.

RUN!

And run, we did.

* * * * *

It's amazing how fast a person can run when they think they've become the bull's-eye for a rhinoceros dartboard. Forget jet engines, forget rockets . . . just put someone in front of a good old-fashioned charging rhino and watch them take off.

To be honest, I don't remember how fast or long we ran. All I remember was a never-ending blur of African bush and the sound of my

". . . hhhhh . . ."

screaming. It would have been my more popular

"AUGHHHHHHH!"

but when you're running faster than the speed of sound.

"...hhhhh..."

is all you can hear.

In no time flat (or about five hours and twenty-three minutes, if you want to be more exact), we crested a hill and looked down upon a huge city below us.

"Wow!" I panted.

Nod, Tomba nodded.

And with that bit of in-depth conversation, we started down the hill into the

"AUG..."

(Sorry, that was the rest of my scream catching up with us.)

noisy and bustling city.

It was a lot like every other big city I'd been to. Same towering buildings, same crowded traffic, same occasional donkey pulling an occasional wooden cart. Well, all right, that part was different, but everything else was pretty much the

HONK! HONK! HONK!

same.

"Get out of the street, you stupid kids!"

See what I mean?

Tomba was the first to spot a policeman standing on a corner. We headed for him.

"Excuse me!" I shouted over the traffic noise. "Excuse me!" He turned to us and I asked, "Can you help me?"

He scowled at Tomba, who stood beside me with his bare feet, wearing his worn gym shorts and ragged T-shirt. "Is this kid bothering you?" he asked me.

"No, sir," I said in surprise. "He's my friend."

The man deepened his frown at Tomba. He seemed pretty unconvinced.

"I'm kinda lost," I said.

"Are you British?"

"No, sir. I'm from America."

"America, huh." He thought a moment, then answered. "The American Embassy is several blocks up this street. If you're lost, I'm sure your parents have contacted them."

He spotted a passing taxi and blew his whistle. The driver slowed to a stop. The two of them jabbered in a language I didn't understand. Then, after shoving some money into the driver's hand, the policeman opened the taxi door for me and I climbed inside. Tomba started to follow, but the policeman held him back.

"You sure you want *him* to come with you?" he asked.

"Yes, sir. Like I said, we're friends."

Reluctantly, he let little Tomba climb inside. He said one last word to the driver, and we were off.

A few minutes later, we came to a stop in front of the American Embassy. I opened the door, got my foot caught on the floor mat, and immediately

"OAFF!"

fell onto the pavement. (Hey, just 'cause we were in civilization didn't mean my coordination had to improve.)

Tomba helped me to my feet, and we shut the taxi door. Before we could thank the driver, he took off in a thick cloud of

"Cough, gag, cough,
choke, gag, choke!"

smoke.

When the air finally cleared (not to mention

our lungs), we looked up and saw a giant iron gate across the street and a sign that read:

AMERICAN EMBASSY

We threaded our way through the traffic, enjoying more of the usual number of cars honking and nearly hitting us, until we arrived at the gate.

Two American soldiers stood on each side. I approached one who was just a couple of years older than Brock (or was it Burt?—I guess since they're twins it doesn't matter).

"Excuse me," I said.

"What is it, kid?"

"I've lost my parents. The policeman down the street said I should come here."

He looked me over carefully. "You got a passport?"

I searched my pockets but couldn't find anything. "No, sir. I think I lost it."

"Lost it?" He looked even more suspicious. "How?"

"I'm not sure. Maybe the baboons got it."

"Baboons?"

"Yeah, or the hyenas. Or maybe it was that warthog, or the baby elephant and his mother, or the hiccupping hippo, or the charging—"

He held out his hand. "Whoa, there . . . you were attacked by all those animals?"

"Yes, sir."

"Sounds like you've had a rough go of it."

"Not really. Not if you've read any of my other books."

He paused again to look me over. Finally, he called to his partner. "O'Riley?"

The other soldier approached. "Sir?"

"Take this kid inside. See if his parents have been looking for him."

"Yes, sir." The second soldier motioned for me to follow.

Suddenly, I remembered Tomba. "Wait a minute. What about him?" I asked.

"What about him?" the first soldier said.

"He can come with me, right?"

The soldier shook his head.

"But he's my friend."

The soldier looked sternly at Tomba. Like the policeman down the street, he seemed pretty suspicious of how Tomba appeared in his worn clothes and bare feet. Finally, he answered. "If this little guy's your friend . . ."

"Yes, sir?"

". . . then I'd be more careful who you choose as your friends."

"Let's go, son." The other soldier moved me forward.

"But," I said turning to argue, "he saved my life."

"Look, kid, do you want inside or not?"

"Well, yeah, but—"

"Then you come in, and he stays out."

I looked at Tomba with concern. But he nodded for me to go ahead. It was like he was used to being treated this way. Like because he was poor and everything, he was used to it happening.

Maybe he was.

I passed through the gate and started up the building steps. Then, turning back to him, I shouted, "I'll be back, Tomba. I promise, I'll be back."

The little guy gave me that great big smile of his and nodded.

Chapter 10

Wrapping Up

About an hour later, I was sitting in the Embassy hallway when I looked up and saw my family coming toward me. I leaped to my feet and did the required trip-over-the-rug routine (which called for the required

*K-thudd*ing

on my face).

Once I got those formalities out of the way, I ran down the corridor toward them, shouting, "Dad!"

"Wally!" Dad yelled back.

"Mom!"

"Wally!" Mom yelled.

"Carrie!"

"Wally!" Carrie yelled.

"Burt and Brock!"

"Way to go, dorkface."

(Isn't it nice to know some things never change?)

Of course, Dad tried to be all cool and manly and everything . . . while Mom kissed me so many times I thought my face was going to get blisters. And when she wasn't kissing me, she was asking me so many questions I thought I'd go deaf (or began wishing that I could). . . .

"Wally, what happened? Wally, are you all right? What did you do to your feet? Where did you get those shoes?"

"I'm okay," I said, gasping for breath between kisses. "Really, I'm all right; everything's perfectly normal."

"If he's perfectly normal, then something's majorly wrong," Brock (or was it Burt?) said, smirking.

I started telling everyone about all of my adventures, including the attack on the village.

"It sounds pretty serious," Dad said.

I nodded. "It is. We gotta go back. We gotta help them."

"We'll see," Dad said. "But right now we need to get you to a good hotel, get those feet cleaned up, and have some decent food."

"All right!" Burt and Brock high-fived. "A hotel!"

"But what about the village?" I asked.

"We'll tell Diggers. Maybe next time he can—"

"Next time?? What about now?!"

"Son, you said yourself you don't even know where this village is."

"But Tomba does. Come on!" I grabbed his hand and dragged everyone back down the hall and out the door. But when we got to the gate, there was no Tomba.

"Where is he?" I asked the soldier.

"Who?"

"The little kid who was with me."

"The police told him he had to move on. Said he was an eyesore."

"An eyesore!?" My heart sank. I looked up and down the street. "But . . . I've still got his shoes."

"Those are *his* shoes?" Mom asked.

"Yes, he gave them to me. But it wasn't a big deal for him. In fact, he was kinda happy to do it. It's like the whole village, they were always happy doing things like that. Even though they didn't have stuff, they seemed happy."

Dad gave me a little smile. "Even though they didn't have things, they were happy?"

"Yeah, how weird is that?" I shrugged. "In fact, in some ways they were even happier than us."

I looked up to see Dad's smile turning into a

grin. "Sounds like you may have learned a lot more than how to run from wild animals."

Now, to be honest, I wasn't exactly sure what he meant . . . though I suspected it had something to do with why we took this trip in the first place.

Anyway, after filling out a bunch of papers at the Embassy, we all crammed into a taxi and started for the hotel. I wasn't crazy about not finding Tomba. I was even less crazy about hanging out in some fancy hotel when there were so many people who needed our help.

"What about Diggers?" I asked. "Weren't we supposed to pass out food with him?"

"We already did," Mom said. "The people were so desperate, it was gone in the first few hours."

"So there's nothing I can do?"

"It's already been done, Sweetheart."

I gave a heavy sigh, then leaned back in the seat. The past twenty-four hours hadn't exactly gone the way I'd planned. Finally, to take my mind off the disappointment, I dug out Ol' Betsy and went back to work on my superhero story. . . .

When we last left Rhyming Dude, he was being seduced with the books of Dr. Seuss.

```
"Hey, you just made a rhyme,
And for a kid author, it's
    pretty fine."
```

"Thanks, dude." I typed. "But you're supposed to be under Material Man's spell of greed, remember?"

```
"But do you think that will sell,
Me being under his spell?
Because if I'm right,
Isn't this where we fight?"
```

"Don't worry, I have it all under control. Now, if you don't mind, let's wrap up . . ."

```
"You're the writer."
```

"That's right."

```
Our hero nods and continues reaching
for the books. Closer and closer he
comes. He sees only the books. He dreams
only of owning them. He wants only to—
```

```
"Excuse me, I don't want to
    be a jerk,
But do you really think that
    this will work?"
```

Ignoring him (and deciding my next superhero story will star someone who can't speak), I gave Material Man another menacing

"Moo-hoo-ha-ha-ha"

laugh.

"Thanks, I was beginning to think you'd forgotten about me."

(Maybe my next bad guy won't speak, either.) But for now...

He continues his menacing materialism by telling our hero, "And to prove there are no hard feelings for all those awful rhymes you've made me listen to, I'll let you have your big-screen TV back, too!"

In a flash, our bad boy motions for one of his servants to wheel in the TV he'd stolen way back on page 19. It's a nice idea, except for the commercial that's playing on it. Well, it really isn't a commercial, it's one of those "Help Feed the Hungry" spots they're always showing. You know the type, with all those starving kids with sticklike arms and legs...and flies.

Now, Rhyming Man has seen these

commercials a hundred times before. But for some reason, this time he really sees them. It's strange, but he *really* sees them.

"Not so strange, Mr. McDoogle,
With all that you've seen
Still running through your
noodle."

Well, whatever the reason, as our hero stares at the screen, the sinister spell suddenly snaps.

"What's going on?" Material Man demands. "What happened?!"

"Look at the people in such need,
All the ones we can't feed,
All the ones you won't heed,
All because of your selfish greed."

"Don't be ridiculous; my greed's not making them hungry."

"But it's your greed that's not fixing it. It's your greed that's stopping you from helping others."

"Hey, wait a minute," Material Man says. "What happened to your rhymes?"

"Sorry, this is too important to fool around with rhymes."

"But that's your thing."

"Not anymore."

"Really?" Material Man asks. "Wow, the next thing you're going to tell me is that the upcoming fight scene isn't important to you, either."

"That's right."

"But that's where you win. That's where you save the day and become the heroically handsome hero."

"I think there are other ways to be a hero."

"Really? Without beating me? Without forcing me to give all my cool stuff away?"

"I think you need to give back the things you've stolen."

"Oh, brother."

"But I think it's okay to have stuff——"

"Oh, great!"

"But it doesn't have to be the biggest, or the best, or the most."

"Oh, really?"

"Really. I mean, there's so many people we could be helping."

"You mean like all those faces on that TV commercial?"

"They're more than faces," Rhyming Dude says. "They're real people with real moms and dads and brothers and sisters."

"Hmm...I guess I never really looked at it that way."

"Think about it. Wouldn't it be cooler to put your money into somebody's life instead of some bigger, fancier gizmo? Wouldn't you be happier saving somebody instead of buying the latest thingamabob that's just going to break down and rust anyway?"

"Well, now, that's a good point. I mean, all thingamabobs eventually rust...but people never do."

"Exactly!"

And so, as we come to another corny ending (that's more than a little preachy)—

"But preachy with a good point," Material Man interrupts.

—(That's preachy with a good point.) The music begins and we roll credits as our two characters continue talking over what they can do to help others.

Eventually, they lock arms and begin strolling into the sunset. All this as Rhyming Dude sacrifices his extremely limited talent for rhyming—

"Hey, I heard that!"

—to help the poor and starving (not to mention sparing the rest of us all the extra ear suffering).

"I heard that, too."

Because any sacrifice we make, no matter how small (or extremely limited), will be a way of doing good for others.

I looked up from Ol' Betsy. It's true, it was a pretty corny ending. (Aren't they all?) But it's also true, it had a pretty good point. I turned and glanced out the taxi window just as we passed some supercheap discount shoe place. Suddenly, I had an idea.

"Wait a minute!" I shouted. "Wait a minute!"

"Now what?" Burt said, sighing.

"What about shoes? Did those people you and Diggers gave the food to have shoes?"

Dad shook his head. "Not that I could see."

"Then let's stop the taxi and buy them some shoes!"

It was Brock's turn to sigh. "With what as money, brainless?"

He had me there . . . but only for a minute. "With the money we save by not staying in a fancy hotel tonight!"

"Yeah, right," Carrie scoffed. "And what about dinner?"

"We could skip that, too!" I exclaimed. Turning to Dad, I asked, "Could we? I mean, we've come all the way here, can't we do some more things?"

Dad glanced at Mom. "Well," he said, "we know Diggers is sleeping in the plane tonight. And he has plenty of antiseptic that we can clean up your feet with. I suppose we could stay with him."

Mom nodded. "And pass out the shoes tomorrow morning before we leave."

After another moment, Dad called out to the driver. "Stop the cab."

"WHAT?!" Burt, Brock, and Carrie cried out in perfect, three-part agony.

As the car slowed to a stop, Dad dished out the money to the driver and said, "Looks like our little mission trip isn't entirely over yet."

As we climbed out of the car, Brock (or was it Burt?) leaned over and whispered in my ear, "You'll pay for this, moron . . . believe me, you'll pay."

I gave a nervous smile (the type condemned prisoners give in front of firing squads)—before we turned and risked our lives crossing the

HONK! HONK!
SQUEAL! SQUEAL!

street to the shoe store.

One thing you could say about Burt and Brock: They always kept their word—especially when it came to doing me bodily harm. Which meant our little shoe-shopping adventure would cost me a lot more than a missed meal or a night in a fancy hotel.

But even that seemed a small price to pay, especially if it meant giving people the help they needed.

And for some strange reason, as we entered the store, I felt my smile growing bigger. It's like I was feeling a joy I hadn't felt before. The type Diggers had talked about. The type I saw on the villagers' faces when they gave me their food, or when little Tomba gave me his shoes.

The type of joy I suspected Mom and Dad wanted us to experience when they first dreamed up this little trip. A joy that they couldn't buy, but that made this the best Christmas present ever.

* * * * *

Oh, and one last thing: It's been a couple of months since our little trip, and I just got this e-mail from Diggers. It's pretty neat, so I figured you'd want to read it . . .

Sent: 22 Feb 4:10 p.m.
From: Diggers
To: Wally McDoogle
Subject: hi

hey, wally!

i just got back from another trip to africa and read your book on the plane. thanks for sending it. very, very cool . . . (except you didn't spend enough time describing how awesomely great i look). oh well, maybe next time. ☺

i also liked the part where material man finally learned his lesson . . . and i guess you did, too! double cool!!

i ran into ben, that village chief you were with, at our latest food drop. he wanted me to say hi and tell you tomba and the rest of the villagers are doing fine. the militia gave them quite a scare but didn't seriously hurt anybody.

now they only have to fight the usual stuff . . .
starvation and disease.

listen, i've got a great idea. if any of the kids
reading your book feel like they want to help folks
similar to ben and his village, have them contact
your Wally McDoogle Fan Club on the internet. that
way you can send them links to cool ministries that
will tell them how they can donate money and stuff
to help.

that's all i know, bro. stay cool, and keep blessing
God by blessing others!

see ya,
diggers

_____

So there you have it . . . another major
mishap turned into a major adventure and an
even majorer (don't try that word on your
English teacher) lesson.

I'll do my best to remember it. You do, too,
okay?

Cool.

Guys (and Guyettes)!

Want to hear from me,
the Human Walking Disaster Area,
each week about more misadventures
and the stuff I'm learning in the Bible?

There'll also be riddles to solve
and chances to win prizes!

Log onto www.BillMyers.com and click
on the Wally McDoogle Fan Club icon for
more information and how to join!

Hope to hear from ya!

Wally